Steve Barlow and Steve Skidmore

Illustrated by Santy Gutiérrez

LONDON·SYDNEY

Franklin Watts
First published in Great Britain in 2019 by The Watts Publishing Group

Credits
Series Editor: Adrian Cole
Project Editor:Katie Woolley
Consultant:Jackie Hamley
Designer: Cathryn Gilbert
Illustrations: Santy Gutiérrez

HB ISBN 978 1 4451 5976 8
PB ISBN 978 1 4451 5977 5
Library ebook ISBN 978 1 4451 5978 2

Printed in China

Franklin Watts
An imprint of
Hachette Children's Group
Part of The Watts Publishing Group
Carmelite House
50 Victoria Embankment
London EC4Y 0DZ

An Hachette UK Company
www.hachette.co.uk

www.franklinwatts.co.uk

THE BADDIES

Lord and
Lady Evil

Dr Y

They want to rule the galaxy.

THE GOODIES

Boo Hoo   Jet   Tip

They want to stop them.

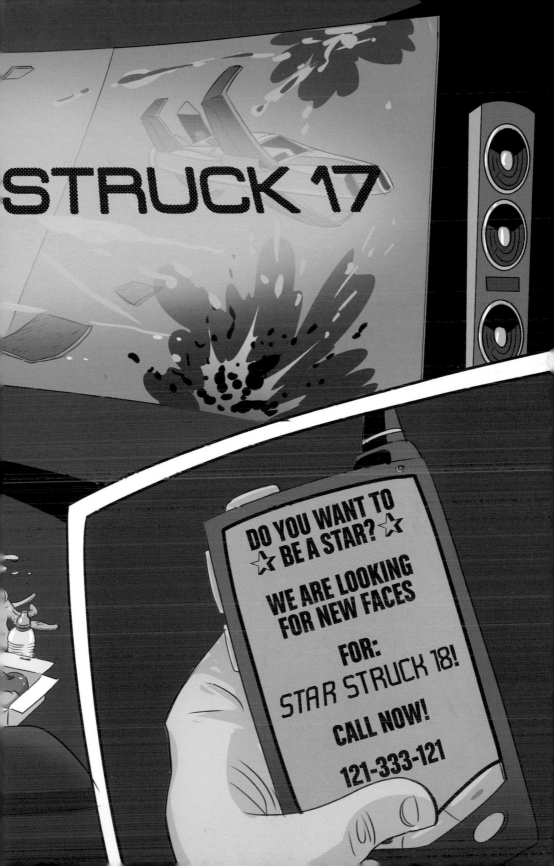

"Look at the stars in it!" said Tip.

"Duke Skyrocket and Bob the Blob..."

"We should try out for it," said Jet.

Boo Hoo smiled. "Are you joking?"

Have you been to Costume and Make-up?
Yeah...
Great! First scene, you have to swing across that pit of Alien Killer Fish.

15

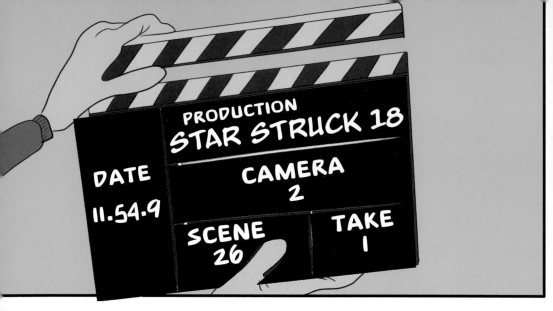

Tip groaned. "I didn't think this would be so dangerous."

"I'm starting to have a bad feeling about this," said Jet.

"It's a dummy!" said Jet. "The movie
is a fake. It's a trap — for us!"
The producer came over. "Next, you
are being chased by these bad guys..."
Jet winked at Tip. "Could you show
us, please?"
"No problem," said the producer.

THE END